Table of Contents

Rourke Educational Media

A Division of Carson Dellosa Education

Can you find these words?

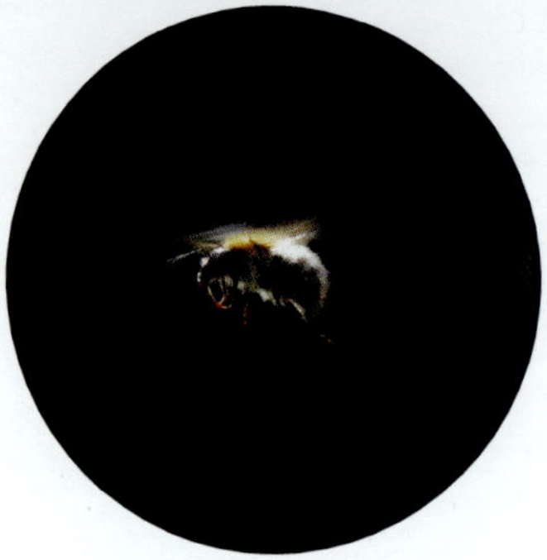

bee

flower

food

hive

Bees Buzz

I hear a buzz. I see a **bee**!

The bee looks for **food**.
The bee sees a garden.

The bee finds food in a red **flower**.

The bee flies to its **hive**.

Many bees live there.

The bee dances. It buzzes.

Other bees watch and listen.
They know where to go!

The bees fly to the garden.

They find food.

The bees fly home.

All bees sleep.

Did you find these words?

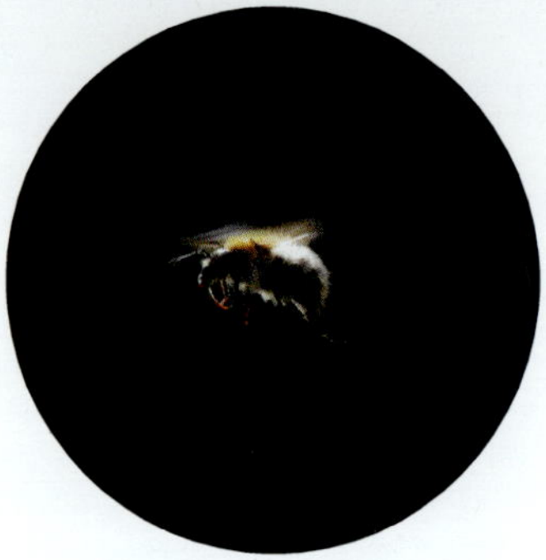

I hear a buzz.
I see a **bee**!

The bee finds food in a red **flower**.

The bee looks for **food**.

The bee flies to its **hive**.

Photo Glossary

bee (bee): A flying insect with four wings that collects pollen to make honey.

flower (FLOU-ur): The colored part of a plant that produces seeds or fruit.

food (food): Any nutritious substance that people or animals eat or drink, or that plants absorb, in order to maintain life.

hive (hive): A natural structure in which bees build a honeycomb.

Index

About the Author

Lisa K. Schnell writes books for children. She also likes to dance, make art, and watch the bees that visit her native plant garden.

www.rourkeeducationalmedia.com

PHOTO CREDITS: Cover: ©StudioSmart; p.2,3,14,15: ©kozorog; p.2,4-5,14,15: ©MirekKijewski; p. 2,6-7,14,15: ©AlesVeluscek; p.8-9: ©zhang bo; p.10-11: ©yuliang11; p.12-13: ©guraydere

Edited by: Keli Sipperley
Cover and interior design by: Rhea Magaro-Wallace

Library of Congress PCN Data
Bees Buzz / Lisa K. Schnell
(Plants, Animals, and People)
ISBN (hard cover)(alk. paper) 978-1-64156-157-0
ISBN (soft cover) 978-1-64156-213-3
ISBN (e-Book) 978-1-64156-268-3
Library of Congress Control Number: 2017957769

Printed in the United States of America
02-1382211937